W9-BHX-897

THE OAK TREE HORROR

ANNE SCHRAFF

 Artesian Press
P.O. Box 355 Buena Park, CA 90621

Take Ten Books
Horror

Other Take Ten Themes:

Mystery
Sports
Adventure
Chillers
Thrillers
Disaster
Fantasy

Project Editor: Dwayne Epstein
Illustrations: Fujiko
Graphic Design: Tony Amaro
©2002 Artesian Press

Artesian **Press**   ISBN 1-58659-073-1

Contents

Chapter 1

Jason Boyd hated big meetings, especially assemblies. Once a week all the students of Wintergreen High pushed and shoved their way into the old auditorium to hear Principal Weems either brag about the school's latest success or, worse, watch her give an award to someone.

As the students sat in their seats, totally bored, someone behind Jason reached out and flicked the back of his ear with a finger. By the time Jason turned around to see who it was, the only thing he saw was a bunch of giggling faces. Jason hated assemblies.

"Okay people, quiet down," Principal Weems's voice boomed through the microphone. "We have some important business to talk about.

"As you all know, the oak tree that

5

stands in the empty field behind the school has been there for many years. I even remember it when I was a student here."

A voice from the back of the room shouted, "Did they have electricity back then?" When the laughter stopped, Principal Weems looked right at Kevin McAllister. His big smile went away when he saw Principal Weems staring at him. When the entire room was quiet again, she whispered into the microphone, "Mr. McAllister, I expect to see you waiting in my office after the assembly."

Like everyone else, Jason looked over his shoulder to watch Kevin's reaction. When he saw that Kevin was sitting only two rows away, Jason knew he was the one who flicked his ear. Kevin rolled his eyes and sighed as the principal spoke to him. His friends nearby teased him.

Jason turned back and looked at the

rest of the students. They all sat in their little groups: athletes, like Larry Goodwin, sat with other athletes, and so on. Jason tried to imagine what it would be like if his class had nerds sitting with athletes, cheerleaders mixed in with Kevin McAllister and his friends, and so on. The thought made him laugh to himself until Principal Weems spoke again.

"As I was saying, the oak tree behind the school has had a long history here at Wintergreen. However, times do change, and with change some things must go. For something good to come to our campus, we must say good-bye to something else. So the oak tree will be coming down to make room for Wintergreen High's brand-new sports complex. To tell you more about it, here is Coach Madison."

Jason couldn't listen to what was being said. He was too shocked by the news that the tree was coming down to hear the words. He loved the old oak tree. He remembered playing catch with his dad under it after school. His mom had made picnic dinners for the family there on the weekends.

Jason's father had been a firefighter. He died saving a woman from a burning building. After that happened, Jason sat under the oak tree and cried where no one could see him. He cried again two years later when his mother died after a long illness.

Now Jason lived with his grandmother. She was loving and thoughtful, but the only living thing Jason ever told his true feelings to was the old oak tree. Now he felt that even the tree was going to leave him.

Jason felt so sad, he thought he might cry. He fought back the tears and tried to listen to Coach Madison's speech. Hearing about the new sports complex, though, only made him think more about the old oak tree.

Pointing his chubby finger at a large drawing of the sports complex, Coach Madison finished by saying, "And this will be the new basketball court. Now, are there any questions? Yes, I believe I see a hand."

Jason looked up and saw Desiree Stern stand up. She asked the coach, "I think it's great that we're getting the sports complex, but is it possible to build it without taking down the tree?"

"I understand your feelings, Miss Stern, but as Principal Weems explained, change often means something has to go," Coach told her.

She sat down with her arms crossed and said to herself, "You didn't answer my question."

As the bell rang to end the assembly, Jason was still sitting, too upset to move. He knew he had to do something to save the tree.

Jason was not very popular in school, mainly because he got good grades and was not into sports. He doubted if he could get enough people on his side to help save the tree, but he had to do something. He thought maybe he could talk to Coach Madison. Maybe Desiree was right. Maybe the sports complex could be built without hurting the tree.

Chapter 2

After school that day, Jason went right to see Coach Madison. As he got closer to the coach's office, he heard a strange sound. It was like a low moan that kept turning into a growl. Jason looked around to see if any stray animals were nearby. All he saw was the old baseball field, his special oak tree, and something lying on the ground under the tree.

When Jason looked closer, he saw that it was a man. Lying on his back with a broken tree branch near his head was Coach Madison. Jason ran to him.

When Jason reached the coach, he saw he had been knocked out. Jason still heard the moaning sound. He looked down and saw a bad cut on Coach Madison's bald head. The coach was breathing, but the moaning was coming from somewhere else. Jason looked up and realized it was coming from the tree.

Feeling a little scared now, Jason stood up and ran to a nearby phone and dialed 911. By the time the ambulance arrived, the coach was beginning to wake up.

After they bandaged the coach's head, the ambulance driver spoke to Jason. They said Coach Madison would probably be okay, but they needed to take him to the hospital so the doctor could look at him.

By now, a crowd had gathered and everyone was talking about what might have happened. Jason listened angrily as they blamed the tree. He was sorry he had not gotten rid of the branch before the ambulance arrived.

The more everyone talked about the tree, the louder the moaning became. Jason wondered if anybody else heard it.

When they put Coach Madison into the ambulance, he cursed at the tree. Everyone laughed but Jason.

As the ambulance drove away, Jason could not hear its wailing siren because of the deafening moan coming from the tree. He held his hands to his ears and shut his eyes. The crowd slowly walked away, laughing and calling Jason names.

Jason stayed by the tree a little while longer as the sun began to go down. He tried to think of what he could do to help the tree, but he couldn't think of anything.

When he thought about asking his Grandmother if she had any ideas, he suddenly remembered he had to go home. He had promised to help her with dinner because her joints were hurting again. Feeling a little silly, he apologized to the tree and then thought that everyone was right for calling him a weirdo.

As Jason began to walk away, he thought he heard the moaning again. He turned around and saw a low-hanging branch twisting, as if it were in pain. Then, just as suddenly, it went back to normal. Jason shrugged his shoulders and said, "Must be the wind." That's what he *wanted* to believe.

"Hey, Weirdo, are you talking to your only friend again?" Jason looked and saw Kevin McAllister's pimpled face. Standing beside him was Lester Rimes, holding his sides and laughing.

Jason was upset. He knew the whole school would know that he was seen talking to the tree.

Chapter 3

"So, Boyd, are you talking to your friend the tree or what?" Lester said, repeating Kevin's words.

"Nah, I was just carving my initials here," Jason said. He pointed to a spot on the trunk where he had carved "J. B." He hoped they wouldn't notice the initials had been carved almost five years ago.

"You're wasting your time," Kevin snarled. He walked toward Jason. "That tree's coming down soon. Hey, you got any money on you? Lester and I want to get a couple of burgers."

"N-no, I'm broke," Jason said slowly. He hated to admit it was true. Since his parents died, Jason and his grandmother lived in the poor part of town and had very little money.

"You're lying," Kevin said. He

grabbed Jason by his shirt as Lester dug through his pockets. As Kevin stared into Jason's eyes, Lester pulled two nickels and four pennies out of Jason's jacket pocket.

When Kevin saw how little Lester got from him, he shoved Jason away, almost knocking him down. "You're not good for anything," Kevin said. Lester repeated Kevin's words as they walked away, glaring at Jason.

No matter how often it happened, Jason never got used to such treatment. What bothered him the most was that he was almost twice the size of Lester, but he couldn't do anything about it with Kevin standing there.

Not that he even would. Jason was tall, skinny, and looked weak. The only people he ever talked to were his grandmother and Desiree Stern. He told them all about the things he liked most, such as science and math. He was almost ashamed of his good grades.

Everyone else at school seemed to think sports were more important. He told things to Desiree and his grandmother because they didn't make fun of his excitement about discovering new things. They always encouraged him.

He even told them how much he loved studying about rocks and plants. He felt silly at first, but they both told him that what he was studying really was important.

Desiree was with him the day he planted acorns. She told him they would grow bigger than his favorite tree and other kids would enjoy them. The more he thought about it, the more he liked Desiree.

A loud moan above him made Jason forget his thoughts. He stepped back and looked at the trunk of the tree. It almost looked like it was moving slightly, as though it had a heart beating inside.

"Hey, it's not my fault!" Jason

17

*Jason looked at the tree and saw it moving, as
though it had a heatbeating inside.*

shouted at the tree. "I didn't plan to put up the sports complex. I don't even like sports." He felt more foolish than before. He thought Kevin was right. It *was* strange to be talking to a tree.

As the tree continued to moan, Jason remembered something he read in a history book. It said Native Americans believed everything in nature was sacred. When they killed a buffalo, they thanked the great animal for the gift of food from the meat and the warmth from its hide. The native hunters would quietly say, "Thank you, great buffalo, for giving your body to us." Jason thought the Native American hunters would understand how he felt, and he began to feel better about himself.

Suddenly Jason realized maybe there *was* something he could do to save the tree. Jason suddenly thought, *I could write down a request to save the tree and get all the kids to sign it. Yeah, that's it—I'll start a petition!*

19

The strange noise that was coming from the tree got quieter until it stopped completely. Jason put his hands into his jacket pockets and hurried home without looking back. He told himself it was just the wind that made the moaning noise come and go.

As he turned the corner, Jason looked back at the tree. He knew it wasn't the wind. He knew whenever the tree heard somebody say something bad about it, it moaned in pain. He also knew how much the tree wanted to live and that it would fight against anything that wanted to destroy it.

Chapter 4

Early the next morning, Jason stood nervously under the tree with his petition—his own written plan to save the tree. He had written it the night before on the used computer his grandmother had saved for so long to buy for him. Jason read books about computers and was able to figure out on his own how to keep it running.

Almost everyone who walked by paid no attention to Jason's petition. He was too shy to ask anyone to sign, and he began to think it wasn't such a great idea after all. That was when Jason saw the most popular kid in school, Larry Goodwin, walk by with his usual crowd of girls who thought he was cool.

A scary thought crossed Jason's mind. Since Larry was so popular, if

Jason could just get Larry's signature, everybody else was sure to sign. Larry was the star of the basketball team and even Coach Madison looked up to the over six-foot-tall giant. What scared Jason was the idea of asking Larry. They had known each other since grade school but had never spoken.

"I hear you got a petition to keep the sports complex from going up," a deep voice said. Standing in front of Jason, with his arm around a pretty cheerleader, was Larry Goodwin.

"Well, it's to save the tree, really," Jason managed to say. "They could put the sports complex somewhere else."

"You heard Principal Weems," Larry said angrily. "There is no place else. That's why the school has no team spirit, Boyd. It's because of people like you and this stupid petition." Larry's arm knocked the clipboard with the petition out of Jason's hands.

Staying brave, Jason picked up the

petition and said, "The complex can go anywhere else. This tree has roots here and has been around longer than just about anything else."

Larry put his face close to Jason's and said, "So are cockroaches but they get stomped on, just like any other useless creature." As Jason felt Larry's hot breath on his face, he also heard a low moan rumbling through the tree.

Just then, Desiree Stern walked up and said quietly, "I'll sign your petition, Jason." All eyes turned to the pretty girl with the dark-brown hair who was just as tall and shy as Jason. Jason handed her the clipboard.

As she signed her name, Larry looked at them both and said, "You two are just plain weird."

"You got that right," said Kevin McAllister. He and Lester walked up to the small crowd gathered around the tree. When Kevin put his arm around Larry, Larry stared at him until he

23

pulled his arm back.

"How about these two, huh?" Kevin said. "I think Boyd loves his tree so much because he's just like one of the cockroaches that lives in it. They shouldn't just take the tree down. They ought to spray it to kill all the little Jasons crawling around in there."

"Jason's not a cockroach!" Desiree shouted. "If anyone's like a little bug, you are, Kevin McAllister! Especially the way you take other people's money and try to make people think you're friends with Larry Goodwin." Everyone stared at the normally quiet Desiree. She kept yelling as if she'd never stop.

"You may not know it," she continued, "but even cockroaches like you serve a purpose. To destroy them would be bad for the cycle of nature."

Jason looked at Desiree as if he were seeing her for the first time. The crowd walked away as Desiree turned and saw Jason staring at her.

24

"What are you staring at?" she said with a shy smile. When Jason didn't answer, Desiree said, "Come on, we're going to be late for Mr. Webb's science class."

Chapter 5

Jason and Desiree got to Mr. Webb's class as everyone was sitting down. The white-haired teacher organized the papers on his desk until he was ready to speak.

Mr. Webb had long ago lost interest in teaching. It wasn't that he didn't love science. It was just that he felt as though he were doing more baby-sitting than teaching. He simply went through the process of grading papers and trying to control rude students. It seemed he just wanted to avoid any trouble until he retired.

"Mr. Webb, don't you think it's wrong that the old oak tree will be cut down?" He peered over his glasses and saw Desiree Stern with her hand raised.

"Well, don't you?" she asked again. He was too shocked to speak. He didn't plan on getting involved in the growing argument.

"It's, um, not really up to me," he finally said. "Principal Weems has made it very clear that she does not want any of the teachers to say anything about the matter. It's up to the school board, and they've made their decision."

Desiree tried again but finally gave up when Mr. Webb said, "We will now discuss the formation of clouds. That is if it's okay with you, Miss Stern." Knowing she had lost, Desiree rolled her eyes and slumped in her seat.

While Mr. Webb and Desiree were talking, Jason could hear the moaning in the background again. He realized that whenever anyone said something bad about the tree, the moaning started. He tried to concentrate on Mr. Webb's lecture, but he couldn't.

Before going home that day, Jason walked to the oak tree again. As he got closer, he saw a small building just a few yards from the tree. It looked like some sort of box office or snack stand. *Wow*, he thought angrily, *they're not wasting any time getting that sports complex going.*

The moaning began again, louder than ever. Jason looked sadly at the tree and then suddenly back to the box office building.

He wasn't sure, but he thought he saw something move. He walked toward the new building as the moaning got even louder. He then realized the moaning wasn't from the tree at all. Someone with a familiar voice was screaming inside the box office.

He began to run. When he got to the box office, he shouted, "Hey, who's in there?"

Lester Rimes heard Jason and stopped his screaming. He shouted, "Get us out, please! We're trapped in here with them!"

Jason tried the door but it was locked. He ran to the window and looked in. What he saw sent chills down his spine.

Chapter 6

Huddled in the tiny space inside the box office, near the cash register, were Lester and Kevin. They were covered from head to toe with crawling cockroaches. There were so many of them, the entire white floor was now black with bugs. Jason saw a huge cockroach crawl down the front of Kevin's shirt.

In a panic, Jason tried to open the window, but it was locked. Lester and Kevin's screaming got louder and louder as they swatted at the army of bugs that just kept coming.

Jason ran to get help. He saw the bandaged Coach Madison not too far away.

"Coach! Come quick! " Jason yelled. The coach sprinted toward Jason. By the time Coach reached him, Kevin's and

Jason was shocked to see Kevin and Lester covered with bugs.

Lester's screams had turned into wails, making it difficult for Coach to hear what Jason was trying to say. Jason gave up and grabbed Coach's hand and pulled him toward the box office building.

When they got there, the whole front door was now black with crawling cockroaches. Coach searched for his master key and tried but could not open the door. While he tried, Jason saw that the line of bugs was coming straight from the oak tree.

By this time, a big crowd had gathered. Finally, the school's janitor arrived and unlocked the door. When it opened, everyone ran screaming as hundreds of bugs came crawling out. Only Jason saw the roaches crawl back up through the tree's trunk.

Lester and Kevin stood shaking with fright. "What exactly did you boys think you were doing in there?" Coach asked with a frown.

Kevin changed the subject quickly saying, "It's Boyd's fault. He put those roaches in there and locked the door."

Coach Madison sighed. "I'm going to ask you just *one* more time. What were you two doing in there?"

Lester cut Kevin off by saying, "Larry Goodwin left his jacket here and asked us to get it for him."

Larry, who was in the crowd, walked up to Lester. "I'm wearing my jacket, you little liar!" he said to the frightened boys.

When Larry spoke, Coach suddenly knew what had happened. "You two aren't stupid enough to break in there to try to steal money from the register, are you?" Coach asked. "Because there's no money in there yet!"

Lester and Kevin just stared at their sneakers as Coach spoke.

While all this was going on, Jason kept staring at the tree. The bugs had crawled inside, completely out of sight.

It seemed to Jason that the tree had the will to live, and it meant to do just that.

After the excitement was over and Lester and Kevin were taken away, Jason went to Mr. Webb's room. When he got there, Mr. Webb was busy grading papers, including Jason's.

"Well, hello, Mr. Boyd," Mr. Webb said without looking up. "I was just grading your paper on the balance of the ecosystem. Very well done, I must say."

"Thank you, Mr. Webb," Jason said, almost embarrassed by the praise. "Speaking of the ecosystem, don't you think it would be better to keep the tree?" Jason added, "After all, living creatures like birds and bugs depend on the tree and that's all part of the delicate balance of the ecosystem, isn't it?"

Mr. Webb sighed out loud. "Not the tree business again. Look, Jason, you have a wonderful mind. Why not put it to good use and worry about things you *can* do something about."

Without thinking, Jason said, "But the tree doesn't want to die!" Before Mr. Webb could say anything, Jason said he was sorry.

"You have a great future ahead of you, Jason," Mr. Webb said. "Don't waste your time getting involved in things you know nothing about. The tree's future has been decided. Now, I'll hear no more about it."

Jason left Mr. Webb's room and stood by the tree again. He was more sure now than ever that the tree didn't want to die. He was scared when he thought what might happen when the tree was taken down. He knew in his heart the tree would put up the fight of its life.

Chapter 7

When Jason got home that night, he smelled pork chops cooking. His grandmother was preparing dinner in the kitchen. Jason went over to her and kissed her cheek. "How was school today?" she asked smiling.

"I think I got an A on my science paper," Jason said. Before she could praise his good work, Jason added, "They're going to chop down the old oak tree, Grandma."

"Oh sweetheart, how awful," she said sadly. She comforted Jason during dinner as he told her about the sports complex and his petition.

He was careful not to tell her about the roaches or the strange noises the tree made. He wasn't sure she'd believe him. A moaning tree that sent out cockroaches to scare people didn't sound believable, even to Jason.

After dinner, Jason lay down on his bed and tried to think of some way to save the tree. The more he thought about it, the more frustrated he became. Finally, he drifted off to sleep.

Jason woke up all of a sudden a few hours later. Loud, strange noises were coming through the window. Still sleepy and dressed in his school clothes, he climbed out the window and followed the noise. It seemed to be coming from the school. As he got closer, the noises got even louder. Turning the corner to the school's entrance, Jason stood in horror.

The night sky was bright with lights that circled the oak tree. Nearby, men wearing hard hats and holding roaring chainsaws were marching toward the tree. As they got closer, the huge tree waved its many branches like long arms. The chainsaws began to cut into the tree. Its moaning became a scream that made Jason cover his ears. He tried to look away but couldn't.

As the chewed-up wood flew into the air and fell down on Jason, he saw the most terrible sight of his young life. When the branches fell off, blood squirted out of the wailing tree. It was as though its arms were being torn away. Jason screamed at the top of his lungs.

That's when he *really* woke up, huffing and puffing. His grandmother stood beside his bed and said, "Jason, you had a nightmare. What was it?"

Jason was covered with sweat and couldn't speak. It was the most realistic dream he ever had. Exhausted, he flopped down on his bed.

The next morning, Jason saw a bunch of construction equipment and trucks parked at the school. Near the tree was a group of men wearing hard hats, talking very seriously to each other. Jason rushed up to one man and asked what was going on.

"Well, son, we're going to take this old tree down tomorrow to make room for a sports complex," the big man told him.

"How?" Jason asked nervously.

"Interested in construction work, are you?" the man smiled. "Well, I'll tell you. First, we get what's called a cherry picker up here to take the top of the tree off. Then we start cutting the branches and putting the pieces into a wood chipper. When that's done, we go for the trunk . . . hey, kid, why are you running away?"

Jason ran to find Desiree. He didn't have to run far because she was walking toward the tree to see what was going on. Catching his breath, he began to tell her about his dream. The moaning began again, and Jason asked if Desiree heard it, too.

She shrugged her shoulders and said, "It's just all these trucks and everything, Jason."

Just as Jason was about to tell her what the construction man said, Principal Weems walked up to them. "Mr. Boyd, I understand you have a little petition going around about our tree." Jason turned around as Principal Weems spoke. "You've also been talking around school about trying to stop our progress. Well, I won't allow that. If you want to talk to someone about the tree, you can speak to me. It was my idea to get the school board to approve our plans."

"I can pass around a petition if I want to," Jason said. "I might only be a student here but . . ."

Principal Weems pointed a long, skinny finger at Jason to quiet him. "You listen to me," she said with a serious tone. "I said *no more petitions.*"

Suddenly, two huge crows flew out of the tree's thick leaves and began to peck at Principal Weems. Covering her head with her hands, she ran away screaming for help. Jason and Desiree watched in shock.

Desiree then leaned over and whispered in Jason's ear, "I hear the moaning, too, Jason. I've heard it for days. I was just too scared by it to say anything."

Glad that he wasn't hearing things, Jason smiled at Desiree. His smile faded quickly when he remembered his dream. "What are we going to do, Des? We have to save the tree. What on earth are we going to do?"

Chapter 8

That afternoon, a local TV news helicopter flew overhead, following a car chase. It gave Jason an idea. He went to a pay phone and got the phone number of the TV station from the operator.

He called the station and asked to talk to Amilee Hawes, the woman who always did reports about the environment. A few minutes later, he was surprised to actually talk to her. He told her about the tree, and she said she would be right over with a cameraman.

When she and her cameraman showed up, they met Jason by the old oak tree. She was holding a microphone when she introduced herself to Jason. "So how old is this beautiful tree?" she asked.

"I'm not really sure," Jason told her.

"But everybody knows about it, especially people who have lived around here a very long time."

Jason was nervous at first, but the more questions he was asked, the more relaxed he became. After almost twenty minutes of talking about the tree and the sports complex, he asked Amilee when she would start the interview.

She smiled and said, "I think if you watch the 6:30 news tonight, you'll see we did a pretty good job. Thanks a lot, Jason. We'll talk again soon."

Jason stood by the tree as the reporter and cameraman left as quickly as they had come. He shrugged his shoulders and decided just to go home and tell his grandmother about it.

At exactly 6:30, after Jason and his grandmother had dinner, they sat in front of the TV. The tree was mentioned right away, but it was nearly a half hour later that they saw Amilee Hawes.

When she finally did appear, she

43

told most of the story herself, even using some of Jason's own words to describe the situation. Jason was on TV for just a few minutes. As he watched himself, he wished someone had told him to comb his hair.

"I read something that Abraham Lincoln once said," Jason heard himself say on TV. "Lincoln said 'true character is like a tree and reputation is the shadow the tree casts.' I think the school board would be smart to remember that. If they do keep the tree, it would be a good symbol of what true character is really all about."

Jason's grandmother looked at him proudly and said, "That was very well said, sweetheart." Jason blushed.

"We'll be following this story as it develops," Amilee Hawes said. "And now the sports."

He tried, but Jason couldn't hide his disappointment. Most of what he said about the tree wasn't even used, and he thought he looked kind of goofy on TV.

His grandmother knew how he felt and said, "I think you looked very handsome. Besides, you tried your best, and that's all anybody can do."

The next day at school, several students came up to Jason and said they saw him on TV. Many of them signed his petition, but it still wasn't nearly enough to save the tree. Jason knew the school board would just laugh at it.

After the first class of the day ended, Principal Weems walked up to Jason. "You know that camera crew had no right to be on school property without my permission, Mr. Boyd," she said. Her voice was low and angry. "You've put me in a very bad spot. How am I supposed to explain this to the school board?"

"Maybe," Jason said, "you can say that a student of Wintergreen was exercising his First Amendment rights of free speech—something he learned in civics class."

Principal Weems looked so angry it was almost scary. She got very close to Jason and whispered, "You listen to me, young man. You do not know with whom you are dealing here. You are *not* going to ruin my plans for this school's future. One more stunt like that and you will be kicked out of school for two weeks. That tree is coming down at the end of the school day, and you are going to have to accept that fact. Have I made myself clear?"

Jason swallowed hard and just nodded. Principal Weems's face seemed to return to normal. She ran her hand through her hair, turned, and walked away. Several feet away, the tree moaned sadly.

Chapter 9

After the final bell rang that afternoon, Jason rushed out to the tree. He wasn't sure what he would do, but he hoped he might get an idea. When he got there, the tree was surrounded by a crowd of people, cars, and trucks. Jason saw police cars, fire trucks, construction trucks, people carrying signs, almost all of the students and teachers, and even Amilee Hawes.

As Jason got closer, Amilee ran up to him and stuck her microphone in his face. He couldn't quite hear what she was asking because of all the noise around him.

Jason looked at the huge crowd, searching for Desiree. The whole area was like a carnival, and Jason felt sick thinking it was all his fault.

Suddenly, Principal Weems showed up with several police officers behind her. She walked over to Jason and spoke close to his ear so the reporter couldn't hear her.

"Jason, you've been warned," she said to him. "This entire circus is your fault. I will deal with it, but first things first. You're suspended for two weeks."

She spoke to the officers and ordered some of them to get the reporter off the school grounds. She then told the other officers to take Jason home.

Two police officers held Jason's arms tightly and pushed him through the crowd. Amilee Hawes kept asking Principal Weems what she was afraid of as the policemen took her and her cameraman away.

When Jason was put into the police car, an officer told him, "We're just going to take you home until this is over, kid. Believe me, you're better off."

Once Jason was dropped off at his house, the police again told him to stay there until things returned to normal. After he watched the police car drive around the corner, Jason then began to run back to the school.

As he got closer to the entrance to the school, Jason began to hear something above the noise of the crowd. He felt sick to his stomach when he realized what it was. It was the exact same wailing and noise of chainsaw motors he had heard in his dream.

Desiree ran up to Jason with a scared look in her eyes. "Where have you been, Jason?" she asked. "Principal Weems got the police to clear the area, and they started cutting the tree." Before he could answer, she grabbed his arm and pulled him toward the police line near the tree.

Above the tree, black clouds began to form. Jason looked at the giant oak tree and saw that a third of its huge top

49

had already been cut away. At the base of the tree was a pile of branches that Jason couldn't help thinking looked like a bunch of arms. It made him feel like he wanted to cry.

Mr. Webb stood next to Jason and Desiree. "It looks like a storm's coming," he said. Jason looked up and saw that the clouds were only above the tree. The rest of the area was still bright with sunlight. The sky turned a scary black color as strong winds began blowing leaves, twigs, and other loose objects around.

Jason leaned over to Desiree and said, "The tree knows, Des." She looked at Mr. Webb and then whispered to Jason, "Please don't talk like that, Jason. I like you and I don't want to see you get in any more trouble."

Her words made Jason shiver. Then, as he looked up at the tree again, Jason couldn't hold back his tears.

This time, Jason and Desiree both

heard the terrible, loud wail of the tree as the chainsaws continued to cut it up. The howling wind let Jason hide his crying eyes from Desiree.

Suddenly, with a roar of thunder, a lightening bolt struck. It sent the policemen running for shelter behind their cars, and the construction workers hid by their trucks.

Jason was going to run, too. Something stopped him. Whatever it was held him so tightly his ankle hurt. He looked down and saw the roots of the tree crawling up his leg. The roots quickly covered Jason's entire body.

Chapter 10

Jason shut his eyes and tried hard to get free. He slowly opened one eye and looked up at the tree, scarred and ugly from the chainsaws.

Blinking against the strong winds, Jason saw the construction workers crouching under their trucks and the policemen in their cars. He suddenly heard a strange *rat-a-tat* sound. It came faster and faster and sounded like bullets. Around him, paper and leaves swirled angrily.

That's when he realized the sounds he heard came from something hitting the cars like bullets. He saw acorns falling hard and fast from the tree. They shattered windshields and dented the vehicles, even the huge crane that would be used to take down the tree.

The only person Jason was barely

able to see was Desiree. She stood bravely against the storm and called out to him.

The tree's moaning was now louder than ever. He wanted to cover his ears, but he couldn't move his arms. All he could think about was how he could possibly live through this nightmare.

Huge clouds of leaves, twigs, and papers swirled in front of Jason as the windstorm grew. Suddenly, a piece of paper stuck on one of the remaining branches and slowly moved toward Jason. As it got closer, Jason turned his head away, but another branch reached up and moved his cheek toward the paper.

Jason tried to read the flapping paper. It was a memo on stationery that said Wintergreen Land & Title Company. It looked like a listing of all the business partners that would be owners of the new sports complex. At the very top of the list of owners was

The tree forced Jason to read the flapping paper.

the name of the largest investor, Principal Joanna Weems.

In spite of the angry wind and craziness that surrounded him, Jason felt suddenly calm. He now understood why Principal Weems fought Jason's attempts to keep the tree. She owned the land it stood on and would make a huge amount of money by tearing the tree down.

Desiree continued to yell Jason's name. As her voice was about to give out, the wind suddenly stopped. Too surprised to react, she watched as the roots holding Jason began to unwind. The air was calm and strangely quiet.

Jason was free and fell on the ground. Policemen and construction workers slowly got up from their hiding places, asking themselves what might have caused the strange event. As Desiree helped Jason get up, she noticed his face was very calm.

Jason looked at Desiree and held up

the piece of paper so she could read it. She read it briefly and then gasped out loud. He then walked to where Amilee Hawes was hiding under a truck. He had a new story for her now.

Over the next few months, all anyone talked about at school was the story about Principal Weems and her trial. The tree was mentioned once in awhile but only in the most hushed tones.

At an assembly held for the opening of the sports complex, the whole school board turned out. On the stage with them were Coach Madison, Mr. Webb, and Jason Boyd.

When Jason's name was called, everyone cheered. He stood up and went to the center of the stage to receive a special award, presented by Coach Madison.

"As you all know," Coach said into the microphone, "Jason Boyd is responsible for saving our grand oak tree here at Wintergreen High. He also convinced the school board to make it the centerpiece of our new sports complex."

The crowd clapped again as Coach Madison held up his hand and said, "I just want to add that on a personal note, I owe you an apology, Jason. You opened my eyes to a problem I was unwilling to see. I just want you to know that some of us are never too old to admit when we're wrong."

Mr. Webb grabbed the microphone from the coach and said, "I second that." As they spoke, Jason looked out at the cheering crowd and saw Desiree's smiling face. All of a sudden, Jason no longer hated assemblies.